One Day on the Farm

Written by James Wilding 1 Illustrated by Jaimee Christensen

One day on the farm, 1 crow saw . . .

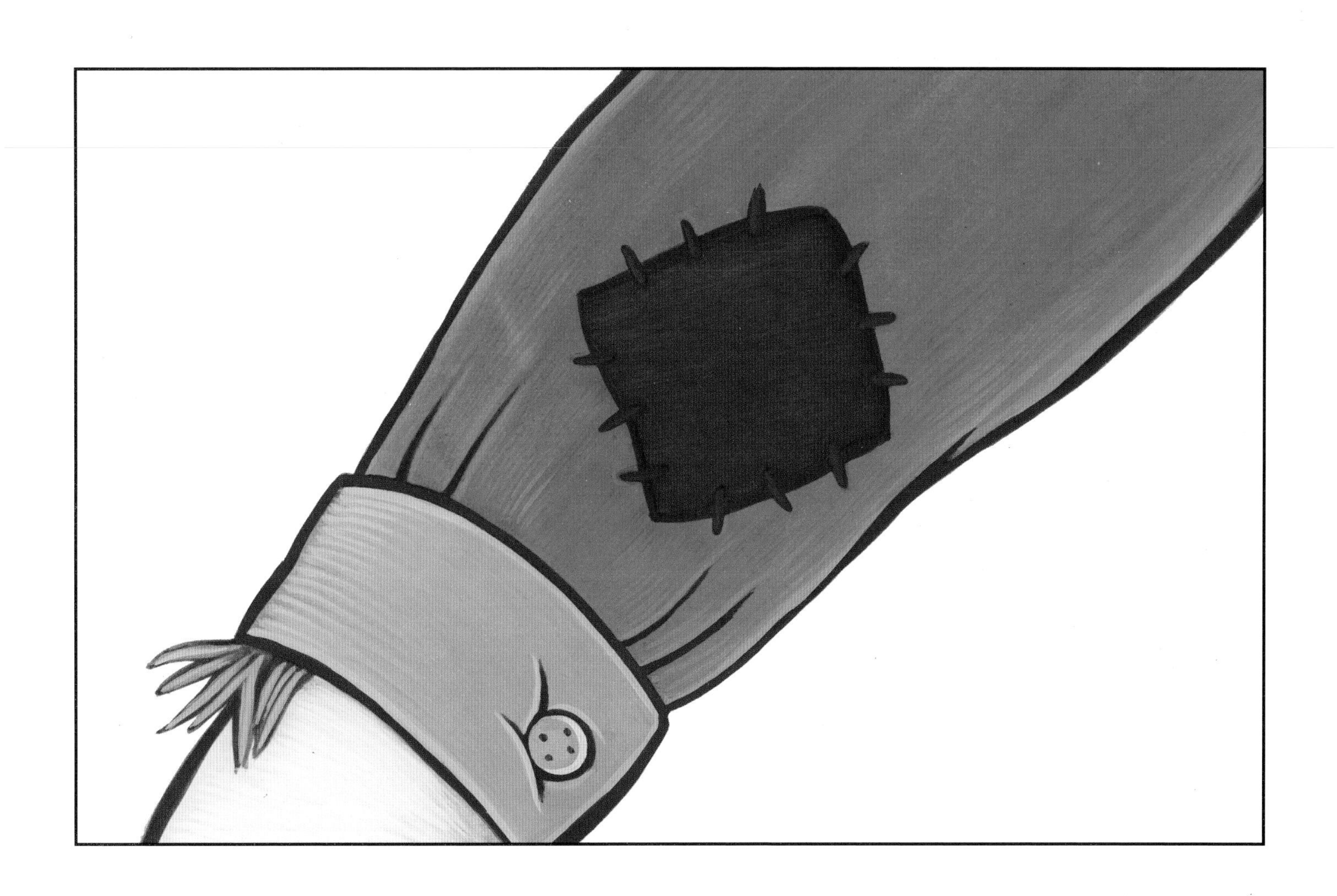

1 red patch, . . .

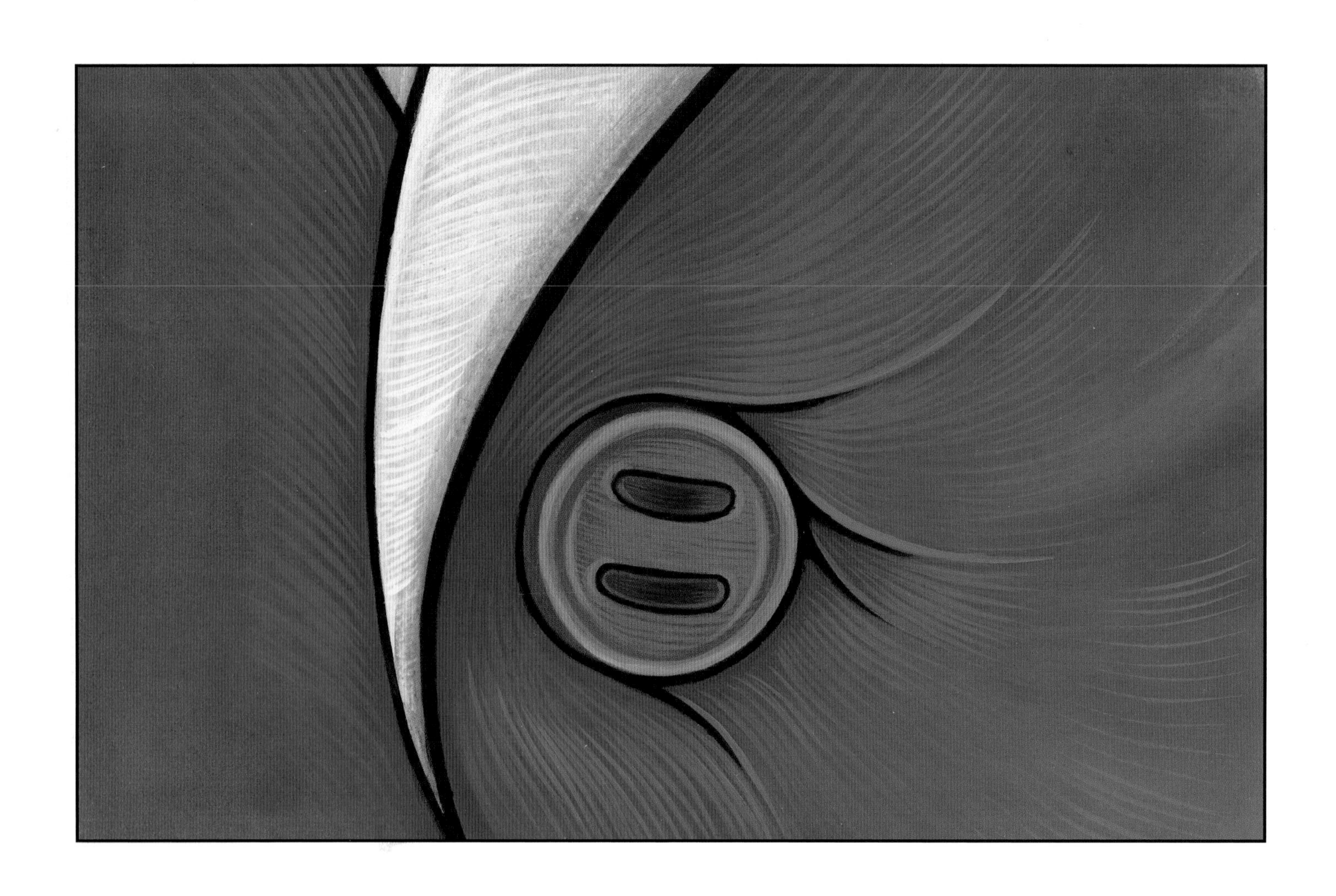

. . . 1 green button, . . .

1 yellow sunflower, . . .

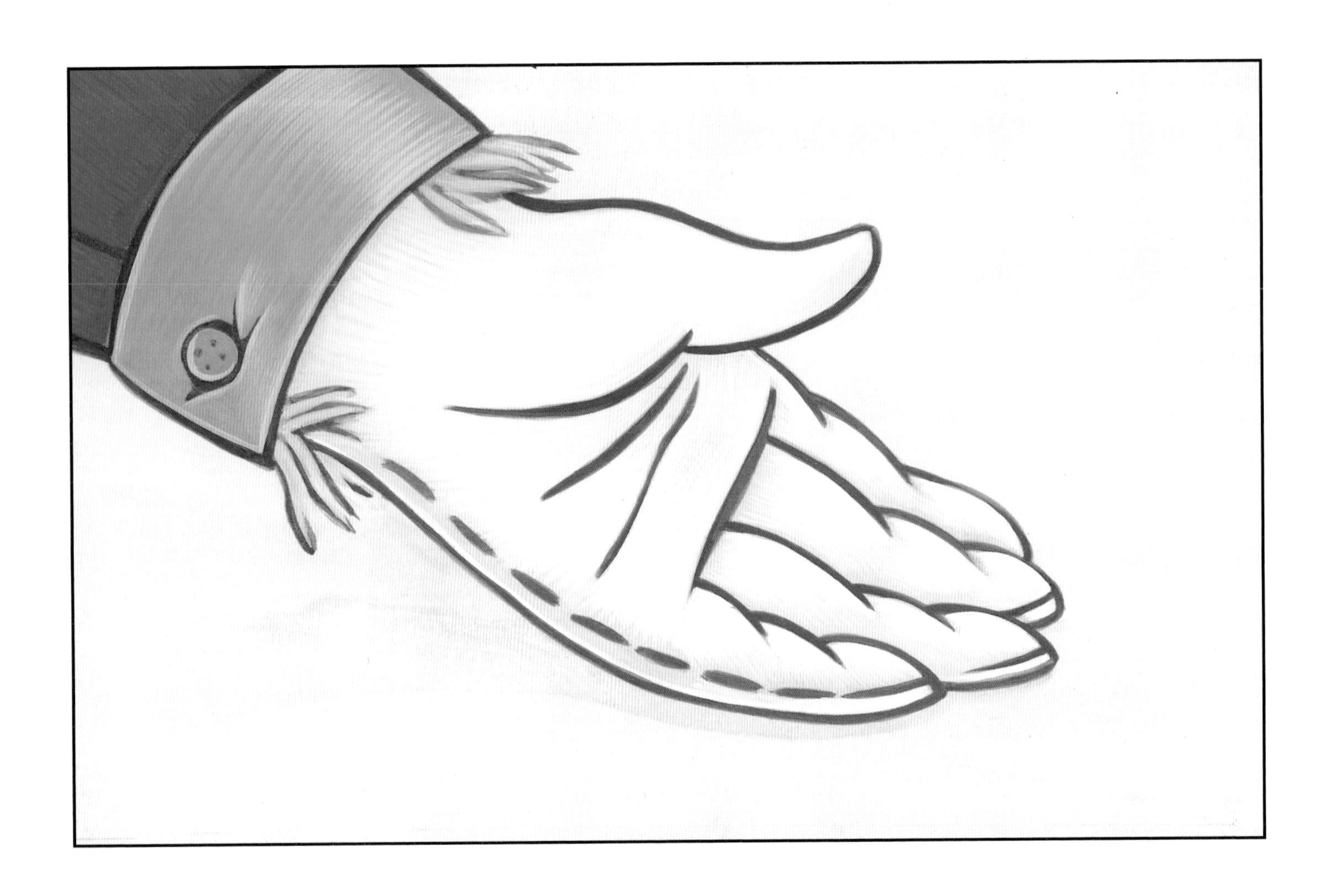

. . . 1 white glove, . . .

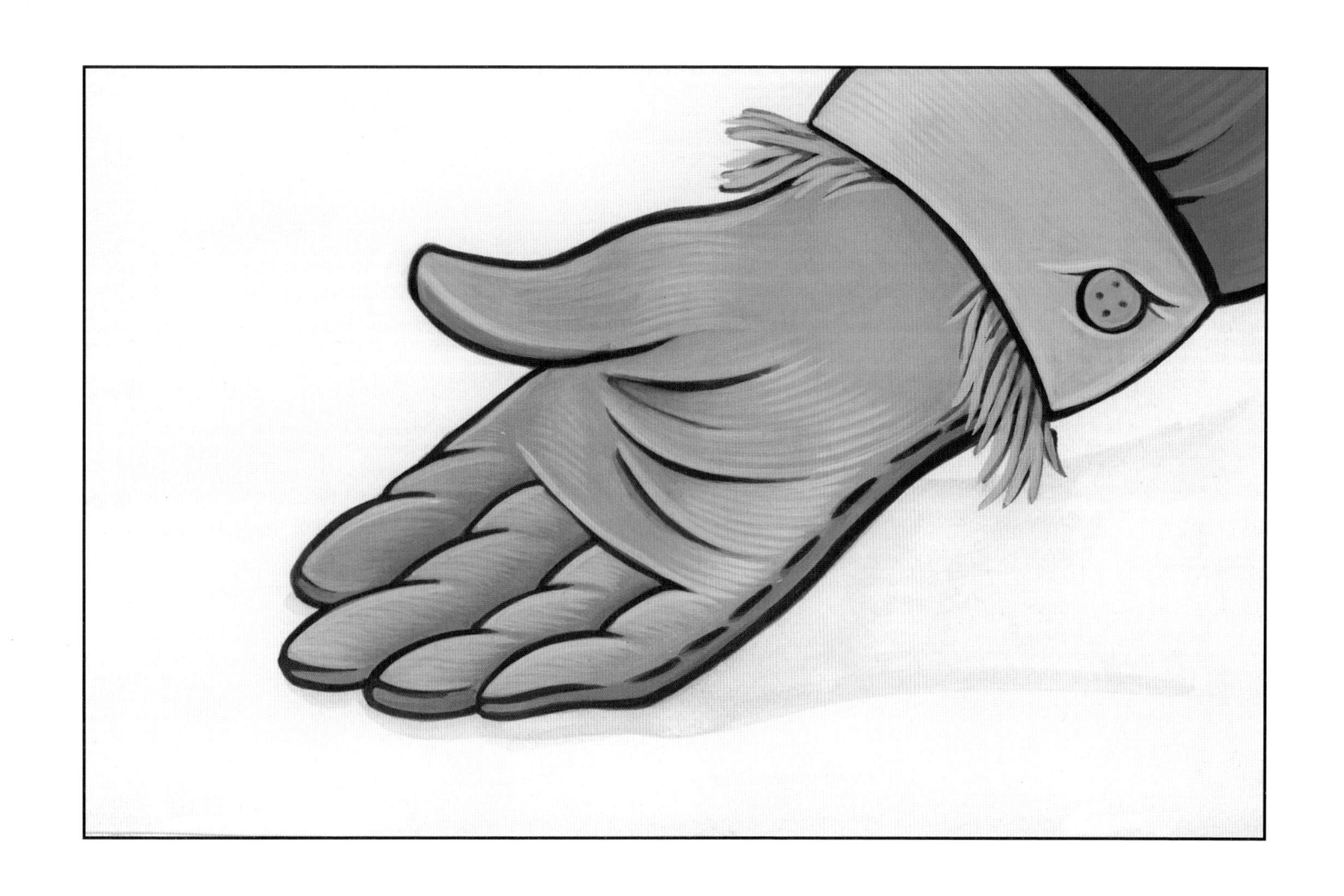

1 gray glove, . . .

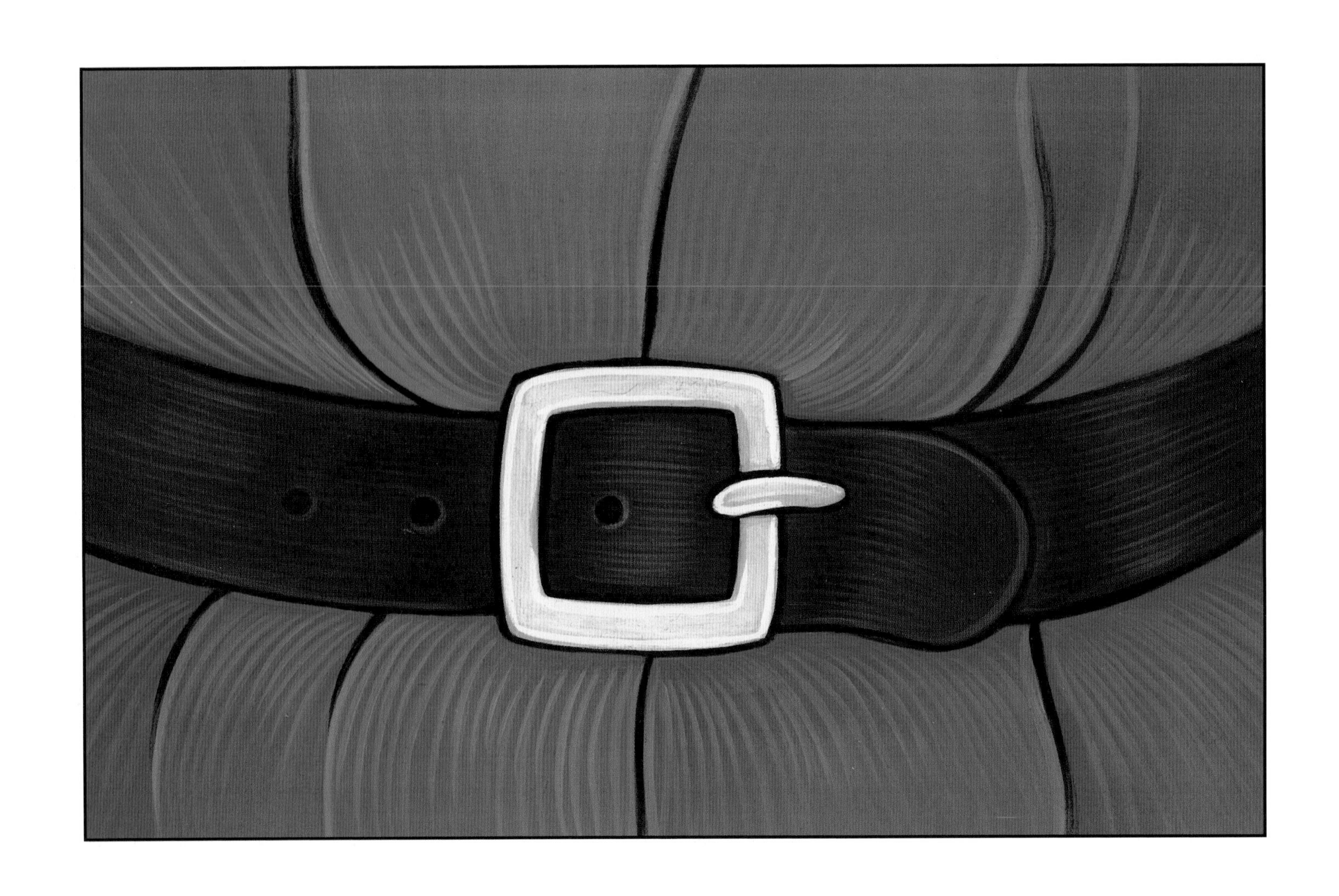

. . . 1 brown belt, . . .

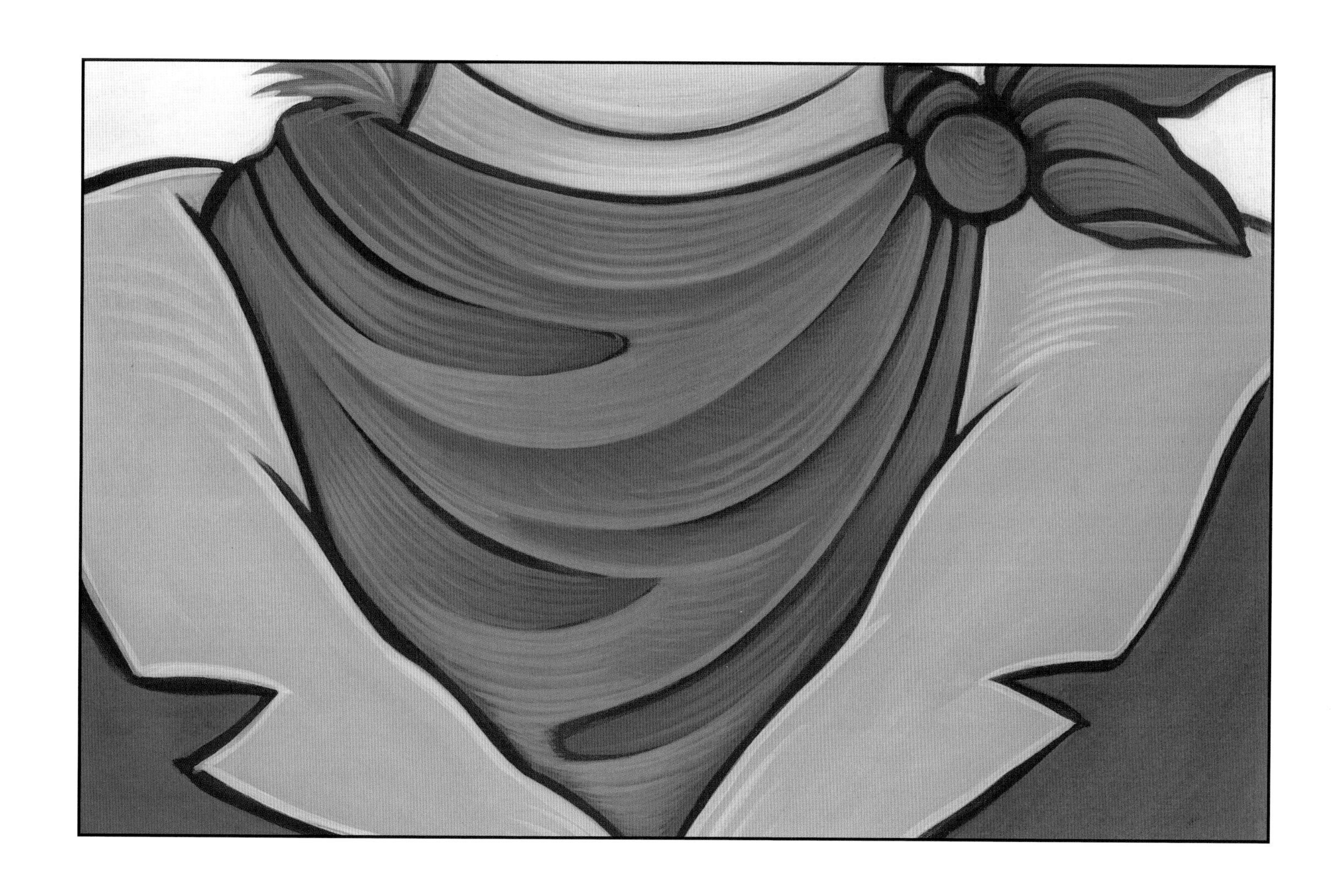

1 purple scarf, . . .

. . . 1 blue coat, . . .

1 straw hat, and . . .

. . . 1 scarecrow!